BMX

Joanne Mattern

Rourke Publishing LLC
Vero Beach, Florida 32964

HERRICK DISTRICT LIBRARY
300 S. River Avenue
Holland, MI 49423

© 2009 Rourke Publishing LLC

All rights reserved. No part of this book may be reproduced or utilized in any form or by any means, electronic or mechanical including photocopying, recording, or by any information storage and retrieval system without permission in writing from the publisher.

www.rourkepublishing.com

PHOTO CREDITS: © Robert Anderson: Title Page; © Giorgio Fochsato: Header; Andreja Donko: page 4; © jallfree: page 5 top; © Renee Brady: page 5 bottom, 7, 8 bottom, 9 top, 18 top, 21; © David Crockett: page 6; © Bostrom Design: page 8 top, 9 bottom, 10, 11, 12, 13, 14, 15, 22; © Ralph125: page 16; © Parema: page 17; © Ames Ferrie: page 18 bottom; © David Maczkowiack: page 19 top; © Raphael Daniaud: page 19 bottom; © Dimitry Zaltman: page 20

Edited by Kelli Hicks

Cover design by Nicola Stratford: bdpublishing.com
Interior design by Renee Brady

Special Thanks to Bostrom Design and Profile Racing, Inc.

Library of Congress Cataloging-in-Publication Data

Mattern, Joanne, 1963-
 BMX / Joanne Mattern.
   p. cm. -- (Action sports)
 ISBN 978-1-60472-394-6 (hardcover)
 ISBN 978-1-60472-805-7 (softcover)
 ISBN 978-1-60472-775-3 (eBook)
 1. Bicycle motocross--Juvenile literature. I. Title.
 GV1049.3.M37 2009
 796.6'2--dc22
                                  2008016351

Rourke Publishing

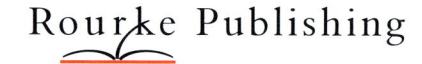

www.rourkepublishing.com – rourke@rourkepublishing.com
Post Office Box 3328, Vero Beach, FL 32964

Table of Contents

What is BMX? 4

The Bike 8

Clothes and Equipment 10

A BMX Race 12

Freestyle Tricks 16

Competitions 20

Glossary 23

Index 24

What is BMX?

Riding a bike is fun. But **BMX** takes bike riding to the extreme! BMX stands for bicycle **motocross**. Motocross is a type of racing done by motorcycles on a dirt track. In the early 1970s, people started copying motorcycle races on their bicycles. They rode their bikes **cross-country**. They rode on dirt **trails**. The bikes flew over bumps and other rough places. Riders jumped in the air and did amazing tricks on their bikes.

Today people of all ages enjoy BMX. They enjoy BMX outside and inside.

Did You Know...
BMX riders do this sport in parks or on special tracks.

There are two kinds of BMX. One kind is BMX racing. BMX racing takes place on tracks. The tracks are at least 1,000 feet (300 meters) long. They have many twists, turns, and jumps.

The other kind of BMX is BMX **freestyle**. There are four types of freestyle. They are street and mini, **vert**, **flatland**, and dirt.

Trick Name: Tailwhip

Freestyle Types

Street and mini: The rider performs tricks on the **pavement** or on **ramps**, walls, and other objects.

Vert: Vert riders do tricks in a **halfpipe** ramp.

Flatland: These riders spin and twist their bikes on flat ground.

Dirt: Dirt-bike riding includes fast speeds, high jumps, and lots of tricks.

The Bike

A BMX bike is not like a regular bike. BMX bikes are tough and easy to **maneuver**.

There are three kinds of BMX bikes. Racing bikes are light and fast. Street bikes and flatland bikes are tougher than racing bikes. These bikes have brakes on the front and rear wheels. They also have pegs on the **axles**. Riders stand on the pegs to do tricks.

BMX bikes also have special wheels. BMX tires are wide. Racing tires are smooth. Street and flatland tires are bumpy.

Clothes and Equipment

BMX riders wear special clothes when they ride. These clothes protect them. Riders must wear helmets. These helmets cover the head, mouth, and chin. Riders who race on dirt tracks also wear a face mask. The mask keeps dirt and dust from flying into their eyes.

BMX riders also wear gloves. These gloves help them hold onto the handlebars. Special shoes help them grip the pedals.

A rider's clothes help to protect his body. Long-sleeve shirts protect the arms. Long pants protect the legs. Riders often wear padded clothes. They might wear pads on their knees, shins, chest, elbows, and wrists too.

A BMX Race

BMX racers line up behind a starting gate. The riders stand up on the pedals. The front wheels of their bikes touch the gate. When the gate goes down, the race begins. Up to eight riders zoom down the track. They must go around **berms**, or turns. They go over jumps too. Some parts of the track are straight and flat. Finally, they reach the finish line. A BMX race only lasts about 45 seconds.

Did You Know...
A BMX race is called a moto.

BMX races are very exciting. Each rider starts out in his own lane. After the race starts, they can change lanes. The riders zoom in and out of the lanes. They try to pass each other to take the lead.

BMX tracks have lots of bumps. Some bumps are close together. Riders call these whoops. Some riders bounce over each bump. Others sail into the air. They fly over all the bumps at once. To jump, a rider pulls up on the handlebars.

Did You Know...

Riders stand as they attack the whoops. Their legs act like shock absorbers.

15

Freestyle Tricks

BMX riders do many tricks. A wheelie is a basic trick. To do a wheelie, the rider pulls up on the handlebars. This pulls up the front wheel. Now the bike rides on just the back wheel. A rider can also do an endo. He rides slowly into a curb or bump. Then the rider leans forward to pull the back wheel off the ground. Riders can also pull up so both wheels leave the ground. This move is the bunnyhop.

Trick Name: Wheelie

Trick Name:
Bunnyhop

Flatland BMX riders do many different tricks. They spin the handlebars. Sometimes they spin the whole bike in the air! Riders also jump off the bike and then jump back on. They push the bike away and then catch it. The rider balances on the pedals or the pegs.

Trick Name: Tailwhip

Trick Name: Backflip Tailwhip

Vert riders use ramps to do amazing tricks. The rider rolls down one side of the ramp. Then he rides up the other side. Riders do tricks in the air.

Did You Know...

Tricks up in the air are called **aerials**.

Trick Name: Turndown

Competitions

There are many different **competitions** for BMX racing and freestyle. Freestyle competitions have judges. Each rider does a set of tricks or a routine. The judge gives the rider points for different things. The rider gets points for his control of the bike, how many tricks he does, and how hard the tricks are. A rider does as many tricks as he can in the time allowed.

Trick Name:
Backflip

Did You Know...

BMX is one of the original sports in the X Games. The X Games feature **extreme sports**.

There are also many BMX racing competitions. Some races are all downhill. Riders fly down the hill as fast as they can. The first one to the bottom wins! Other races have both uphill and downhill sections. Some riders race cross-country. They cover many different kinds of trails.

Stage races combine different kinds of races. A stage race might include uphill and downhill sections and a cross-country race too. Riders get points based on how fast they finish each stage. The rider with the most points wins.

Did You Know...

Some BMX races last twenty-four hours, or a whole day and night! During these races, riders pedal around a course as many times as they can.

Glossary

aerials (AYR-ee-uhl): a trick performed in the air

axles (AK-suhlz): rods in the center of wheels, around which the wheels turn

berms (bermz): turns in a BMX race

BMX (BEE-EM-EX): bicycle motocross; a sport where riders ride bikes over rough trails or pavement

competitions (kom-puh-TIH-shunz): contests

cross-country (KROSS-KUHN-tree): a race run through the countryside

extreme sports (eks-TREME spuhrtz): sports that involve danger and excitement

flatland (FLAT-land): a type of BMX involving tricks done on flat ground

freestyle (FREE-stile): a type of BMX involving tricks and jumps

halfpipe (HAFF-pipe): a U-shaped ramp

maneuver (muh-NOO-ver): to move around something

motocross (MOH-toh-kross): motorcycle racing on dirt tracks

pavement (PAVE-muhnt): a hard material that covers the road

ramps (RAMPS): sloping passageways or roads

stage races (STAGE RAY-sez): BMX races that include different types of tracks

trails (TRALEZ): paths for people to follow

vert (VERT): a type of BMX done on ramps

23

Index

aerial(s)   19
axles   8
berms   12
bunnyhop   16
competitions   20
cross-country   4, 22
endo   16
equipment   21
extreme sports   16
flatland   7, 8, 9, 18
flatland bikes   8
freestyle   7, 16, 20
halfpipe   7
motocross   4

motorcycles   4
pegs   8, 18
racing bikes   8
stage races   22
starting gate   12
street bikes   8
tracks   5, 6, 10, 15
trails   4, 22
tricks   4, 7, 8, 16, 18, 19, 20
vert   7, 19
wheelies   16
whoops   15
X Games   21

Websites to Visit

www.bmxonline.com

www.bmxstunts.com

Further Reading

Doeden, Matt. *BMX Freestyle*. Capstone Press, 2005.

Firestone, Mary. *Extreme Downhill BMX Moves*. Capstone Press, 2005.

Hayhurst, Chris. *Mountain Biking: Get on the Trail*. Rosen Central, 2000.

Herren, Joe and Ron Thomas. *BMX Riding*. Chelsea House, 2003.

Schuette, Sarah L. Downhill BMX. Capstone Press, 2005.

About the Author

Joanne Mattern is the author of more than 300 books for children. She has written about a variety of subjects, including sports, history, animals, and science. She loves bringing nonfiction subjects to life for children! Joanne lives in New York State with her husband, four children, and assorted pets.